Stella Batts

Who's in Charge?

Stella Batts

Who's in Charge?

Book

5

Courtney Sheinmel

Illustrated by Jennifer A. Bell

For all the readers who asked for another Stella story,

especially Maverick C., Priscilla M., and Willa T.

—Courtney

For Lil

—Jennifer

Text Copyright © 2013 Courtney Sheinmel
Illustrations Copyright © 2013 Jennifer A. Bell

Sleeping Bear Press™

2395 South Huron Parkway, Suite 200 • Ann Arbor, MI 48104 • www.sleepingbearpress.com
© Sleeping Bear Press

Band-Aid® is a registered trademark of Johnson & Johnson and its affiliate companies. Cheerios® is a registered trademark of General Mills Inc. Disneyland® is a registered trademark of the Walt Disney Company. PURELL® is a registered trademark of GOJO Industries, Inc.

Printed and bound in the United States.
10 9 8 7 6 5 4 3

Library of Congress Cataloging-in-Publication Data • Sheinmel, Courtney. • Stella Batts : who's in charge? • Courtney Sheinmel ; illustrated by • Jennifer A. Bell. • pages cm. — (Stella Batts ; book 5) • Summary: "Stella volunteers to watch best friend Evie's dog, Bella, for a few days. Disaster strikes when Bella gets loose and runs away. Stella must find her before Evie returns"— Provided by the publisher. • ISBN 978-1-58536-849-5 (hard cover) — ISBN 978-1-58536-850-1 (paperback) • [1. Dogs–Fiction. 2. Lost and found possessions–Fiction.] I. Bell, Jennifer (Jennifer A.), 1977-illustrator. II. Title. III. Title: Who's in charge. • PZ7.S54124Sv 2013 • [Fic]–dc23 • 2013006128

Table of Contents

Free Write

Name: Stella Batts
Grade: 3rd
Teacher: Mrs. Finkel
Assignment: FREE WRITE

Mrs. Finkel says we're having a Free Write, right now. That means we can write about whatever we want. There are no rules. Not even spelling and punctuation count.

Okay, there is one rule: We're not allowed

to stop writing, not even to think. We're just supposed to write whatever pops up in our heads. This is just to get our creative juices flowing. Mrs. Finkel isn't even going to collect our papers.

I could write stellahhhhhhhhhh!!!!!! dov ljlk lkfsu aaaa komeov blah blah blah, if I want.

But I've written FOUR books so far. It shouldn't be too hard to write something better than nonsense words.

Okay, so what should I write?

I know! I'll use this Free Write to start my fifth book. Mrs. Finkel says authors have hunches about what happens in their books even before they sit down to write them.

I have a hunch about . . . oh wait, now Mrs. Finkel is talking. "Eyes on your own paper, Joshua."

Only Joshua could get in trouble during Free Write, when there are barely any rules to break! He gets in trouble a lot, because he doesn't obey Mrs. Finkel's Ground Rules, like "Eyes On Your Own Paper" and "No Calling Out" and "Raise Your Hand Quietly." Also he's the biggest meanie in our class. Want to know how mean? He calls me Smella. Just because of something gross that happened on our class nature walk. It happened at the beginning of the school year, and he still hasn't stopped.

But my hunch doesn't have anything to do with Joshua. My hunch is that maybe my book can be about my new baby brother, Marco! He's soooooo cute.

Here is a list of things that Marco can do:

1.

2.

3.

It's a blank list! He might be cute, but he can't do anything yet!

I help out with him sometimes. Like, I hold him in my lap, sing him to sleep, and even change his diapers—but NOT the gross ones.

Mom and Dad have to do everything else for him, even the gross things. Plus they have work things to do, so they don't get to spend as much time with Penny and me as they used to.

Right now Grandma is staying with us. This morning she took care of Marco, and Mom made breakfast. We had pancakes, in the shape of an S for me and a P for Penny. But actually they looked more like clouds. We were out of chocolate chips, so Mom cut up butterscotch cubes and put them on top.

"Are these from the Penny Candy Wall?" I asked.

"They sure are," Mom said.

The Penny Candy Wall is at Batts Confections, and it's named after Penny. There's also "Stella's Fudge," named for me, and when Mom and Dad think of the right thing, there'll be something for Marco, too.

Except right then Penny said, "I don't want Marco to have a treat at the store."

"Come on, Pen," Mom said. "There's room at the store for Marco to get a treat, too."

"Plus, maybe we'll have to taste-test a bunch of sweets," I told her.

Then Dad came in and said it was time to go to school—he was driving us on his way in to work.

Oops, Mrs. Finkel is clapping her hands now. Free Write time is over. Got to go!

CHAPTER 1

A Step the Word for Me

I decided that this book can't be ALL about Marco, since he's just a baby and he doesn't do anything. So I'll tell you about what happened after school. The bell rang and I headed to the flagpole outside. That's our carpool meeting place. The kids in my school always walk through the hall calmly, but as soon as we get through the door at the end, we all start to run. The teachers can't yell at you to slow down once you're out the door.

Usually I get to the flagpole faster than my friend Evie, who rides with us, because she's always in fancy shoes instead of sneakers. But that day it was warm out so I had on flip-flops. They made a *thwack thwack* sound every time my feet hit the ground. "I can't run because I don't want my shoes to fall off," I told Evie.

She looked down. "I like them," she said. "They're just like a pair that Tesa has."

Tesa is one of Evie's friends from England. That's where Evie used to live.

"Hi, girls," Grandma called. She was standing with Penny. The kindergarteners get out a few minutes earlier than the rest of the school.

"Hi," I called back. It was Grandma's first time driving the carpool, so I had to do some introductions. "This is Evie. She's my best friend in Somers," I said.

Evie is my second-best friend in life. My first-best friend, Willa, moved to Pennsylvania a couple of months ago. I'm really lucky Evie moved here right after that.

"And Evie, this is my grandmother."

"How do you do?" Evie said. Sometimes she talks as fancy as she dresses.

Penny's friend Zoey usually carpools with us, but she had a doctor's appointment, so it was just us three kids, and we all got to sit in back.

"You're like a chauffeur," I told Grandma.

"Tesa and Sara have a chauffeur," Evie said. "Their family is quite rich."

"Are you going to see them in England this weekend?"

"Definitely." Evie's mom is a flight attendant. Usually Evie and her dad stay home when Mrs. King has trips. But they're going to England for the weekend and a couple of extra days. Evie's going to miss Monday and Tuesday of school.

"What do you call their chauffeur?" I asked.

"They call him Sir, so that's what I call him."

I couldn't exactly call Grandma "Sir," since that's for boys only. "Ma'am," I said. "Can you please put on the Barbra Streisand CD?"

Barbra Streisand is a singer that grown-ups listen to, but I like her, too.

"Oh yeah, Gram—I mean, Ma-am Chauffeur," said Penny. "Can you put on 'Step in the Right Direction,' the song Stella was singing yesterday?"

"That's my favorite song," I said.

"Mine too," Penny said.

"Penny, you ALWAYS copy me."

"Do not," she said.

"Do too."

"Come on now, Stella," Grandma said. "Imitation is the sincerest form of flattery." Mom always tells me the exact same thing. She means it's fine that Penny copies me, that it's actually a good thing. But I know she's just saying it so we won't get into a fight. I bet Grandma said the same thing to Mom when Mom was a kid and her little sister, my Aunt Laura, was the one doing all the copying.

My song was about to start. "You're going to love it," I told Evie. I wouldn't mind if she picked it for her favorite song, too. It's different than Penny picking the same favorite. I can't explain why. It just is.

"You are a step the word for me," Penny sang.

"Your voice sounds professional," Evie

told her.

"Hold on," I said. "What did you just say, Penny?"

"You are a step the word for me," she repeated.

"That's not how it goes," I told her.

"Yes, it is."

"No, it's not. It's 'a step *forward* for me,' not 'the word for me.' Your way doesn't even

make any sense."

"It makes the same amount of sense as your way," Penny said.

"Do you have the CD case?" I asked Grandma. She handed it back and I flipped through the little booklet to show Penny the lyrics. "See, it says a step FORWARD." I put my finger under the word to show her.

Penny put her finger right on mine. "*Fff fff*," she started sounding it out, but then she stopped. "I don't know if you're right because I can't read!"

By now the song was almost over. I sang the last bit and tried to hold the notes as long as Barbra Streisand. But she can go much longer without breathing.

"Hey, can I try on your shoes?" Evie asked.

"Sure." Flip-flops are easy to take off. You

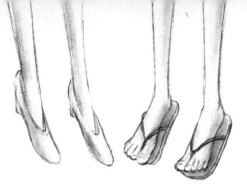

just shake your feet. I shook my feet, the shoes fell off, and I handed them over.

"These fit me rather well," Evie said. The back of her foot was hanging off the shoe, but they still fit her because they were flip-flops. I put her shoes on my feet—sandals with an eensy weensy high heel. I'd never worn high heels before, except for playing dress up with Mom's shoes.

"If I put these on the tightest notch and stuff something into the front of them they'd fit me," I said.

"Let's switch for the weekend," she said.

Evie has an accent so she says weekend like this: wee-KEND.

Grandma pulled up in front of Evie's house. Or not exactly at her house, but on the street right in front of Hilltop Acres, which is the garden apartment complex where Evie lives. Garden Apartments means all the houses are attached but everyone has their own front door. Mrs. King was waiting for her on the sidewalk. She had Bella the puppy with her. Penny and I got out of the car to say hi. Then Grandma got out of the car, too.

"Oh, she's just precious," Grandma said about Bella. I had to agree. The first time I saw her, I wanted her to be mine. I still do, sort of, but having her at Evie's house is the next-best thing.

"Is Bella going away too?" I asked.

"No, our neighbor is watching her," Evie said.

"Actually Mrs. Simpkins had an

emergency, so Bella is headed to the kennel for the weekend."

Mrs. King says "weekend" the regular way, because she's American. I haven't heard Evie's dad say "weekend," but I bet he says it Evie's way, because he's from England, too.

"She can't go to the kennel," Evie said then. "She'll be in a cage the whole time—four days! And what if another, bigger dog is mean to her? We have to take her with us."

"I'm afraid not, sweets," Mrs. King told her. "There are rules against bringing a dog into England."

"Bella could stay at my house," I offered. I knew I should check with Mom or Dad first, but they weren't there and this was an emergency.

"Yeah!" Evie said. "She'll stay with Stella!"

"Stella's family has a new baby," Mrs. King

said.

"It's all right," I said. "The baby won't bother her." Marco can't even lift his head up, so he wouldn't be able to do anything to a dog.

"I wasn't worried about the baby bothering Bella," Mrs. King said with a laugh. "I was worried about Bella bothering the baby, and it's a lot to put on your mom just now."

Grandma was kneeling down, scratching Bella under her chin. "Can you call Mom and

ask if I can watch Bella this weekend?" I asked. "Tell her I'll take care of Bella and feed her and even walk her all on my own." Dogs are NOT Mom's favorite thing. But she wouldn't have to do anything.

Grandma stood back up. "I'll make sure it's okay," she said.

"Really?"

"Of course. Who wouldn't want this little one around?"

Oh boy! A dog of my very own! At least for a few days—I'd get to cuddle her, and sleep with her, and take her for walks, and show her off to everyone who passes by.

Grandma turned to Mrs. King. "She has all her shots, yes?"

"She does," Mrs. King said. "But you don't have to do this."

"You're in a bind," Grandma said, "and

Stella wants to help, so it's settled."

"If you're sure. I have plenty of food you can take along with you. The ID tag on her collar fell off and we're still waiting on the new ones to come in the mail, so just don't let her off the leash. She runs pretty fast."

"I know," I said. "I saw her almost run away one time."

"And you rescued her," Evie said.

"She'll be fine," Grandma said.

"Even better than fine," I said. "We can give her a bath and wash that dirt off her ear."

Bella is all white, like a big, fluffy marshmallow, but now her ear had a little brown on it, like a piece of fudge had smudged it.

"Oh, she's clean," Mrs. King said. "Sometimes dogs get spots as they grow a little bigger. And we won't be gone long, so

you don't have to worry about anything like grooming."

"If you need to stay away longer, I can still watch her," I said.

Evie shook her head. "I don't want to be away from Bella for more than four days."

"I meant just in case," I said. "I'll keep her safe."

CHAPTER 2

Ground Rules
for Dogs

Mom met us at the door with Marco in her arms. He was sleeping, which is one of the few things he can do.

"Did you have nice—" Mom started, but then she interrupted herself. "What is that dog doing here with you?"

"She's Evie's puppy, Bella," I said. "The one Dad, Penny, and I first spotted at Man's Best Friend. You've heard me talk about her."

I was holding Bella's leash with one hand,

and I reached for Marco's hand with the other. Babies have grabby hands, and I like when Marco puts all his fingers around one of mine and squeezes tight.

"Hold it right there, Stel," Mom said. "You know the rule."

The rule is: You have to wash your hands before you touch the baby.

Penny and I had gotten more rules when Marco was born. Parents don't tell you this before you get a baby brother or sister, but they get a bit stricter when the baby comes home.

"Double washing this time since you've touched a dog," Mom said. "And I still need to know what that dog is doing *here*."

"She didn't have anywhere else to go," I explained. "Evie and her parents are going to England until Tuesday, and the lady who was supposed to watch Bella had an emergency."

"Stella," Mom began. "I know you like this dog and you want to do a favor for your friend, but you can't volunteer our house without asking first."

"But . . . but . . . but I can't break my promise to Evie! Then Bella will have to go to the kennel. And besides, Grandma said it would be okay."

"Mother," Mom said. "We have a brand-new baby here." Mom was using the same voice she uses when she's explaining something to Penny and me. "What if the dog jumps up and scratches him?"

"She wouldn't do that," I broke in.

"She's a little dog, Elaine," Grandma added. "How high do you think she can jump?"

Mom made a noise that sounded like

harrumph. "You shouldn't have made a decision like that without asking me first. I don't want to worry about a dog on top of three kids."

"I'll take care of the dog," Grandma said. "You don't have to worry about it."

"You're leaving on Sunday. Who's going to take care of the dog the two days after that?"

"I will," I said. "I'm in charge of her."

"A little responsibility is good for a kid," Grandma added. "Trust me."

At that moment, Bella moved toward Mom's feet and began sniffing them. Dad once told me that sniffing is a dog's way of shaking hands.

But I guess Mom didn't know that, and she jumped back as if Bella was about to bite her. Which, by the way, Bella would NEVER do. Marco's eyes popped open and his forehead wrinkled the way it does when he's about to start screaming.

Mom jiggled him gently up and down. "It's all right, baby. It's all right. I won't let it near you."

"Bella's a girl," I said. "Not an 'it.' And

she's the first dog Marco's ever met, so that makes her extra special." I changed my voice to my baby voice. "Don't you think so, Marco-barko?"

"Wahh," Marco said.

"Here, let me take him," Grandma said. She squirted some Purell on her hands to make them clean, and Mom handed him over. Grandma reached under Marco's pj's and under his diaper to feel—I know, GROSS! "I think he's just wet, Elaine."

Just wet is the kind of diaper I like to change. "Wait for me! I'll do it!"

"Not after touching that dog you won't," Mom said.

Penny tugged on the bottom of Mom's shirt. "What about me? Will you let Bella near me? It's not fair if you just protect Marco."

"I'll protect you both," Mom assured her.

"But Penny, you're too old to need protection from Bella," I said.

Penny shook her head. "I want to go back and be a baby again."

"You can't go back—you can only go forward," I told her. "And that's a good thing, because you get to do stuff like play with dogs. Remember how much fun it was when you were petting Bella the whole way home? But if you talk like that in front of her, she's going to think you don't like her, and that's not how to treat a guest." I paused, and turned to Mom. "She's our guest, right? She can stay?"

"I guess I don't have a choice, do I?"

Why didn't Mom have a choice? Because Grandma was Mom's mom, and she said so? How old do you have to be when you get to stop listening to your mother? When you're as old as Stuart? He's one of the workers at

Batts Confections. Dad calls him a "kid," but he's old enough to be in college and have a job. Mom is even older than Stuart.

"Come on in, girls," Grandma said. "Let's not stand in the doorway."

"Bella too?" I asked.

"Yes, of course."

Mom closed the door behind me and I took off Bella's leash. Penny and I kicked off our shoes, because that's another rule. Mom has been extra strict about it since Marco came. No germs.

"How come Marco doesn't have to take off his shoes?" Penny said.

"He doesn't have real shoes," I told her. "Just booties."

"I think we need to establish some rules," Mom told me.

"Rules like Ground Rules?"

"Yes," Mom said. "The dog is not allowed on the furniture. I don't want her chewing on anything."

"She can chew on food, right?" I asked.

"Food is fine—but just her own food, out of her own bowl. And you have to keep an eye on her—I don't want her wandering around on her own."

"I won't let her out of my sight, I promise."

"She's not to go into the bedrooms," Mom said.

"But she has to go in my room," I said. "I'm going to sleep with her!"

"Fine, your room, but not mine and Dad's, and not Marco's—under any circumstances. Okay?"

"Okay," I said. "Hey Penny, come with me. I'm going to show Bella my room and teach her some new tricks."

Penny shook her head. "I want to stay with Mommy."

"I'm going to lie down for a little bit, now that Grandma has the baby," Mom said.

"I'll lie down with you," Penny told her, even though Penny doesn't usually lie down when she gets home from school. She's five years old—that's too old for naps, if you ask me. But she changed a little bit when the baby came, too.

"I guess it's just us, Bells," I said.

Bella followed me into my room—see, she knew I was in charge of her for the weekend!—and I scooped her up and plopped her on my bed. "This is where you'll sleep tonight," I told her. She sniffed every single one of my stuffed animals. Once she'd met them all, I showed her my dresser and my desk. I showed her all the books I'd already written. Then I put

her on the floor and took a pair of socks from my dresser. They were rolled up so they were like a ball, and I threw them across the room. "Fetch, girl!" I called. Bella trotted across the room, picked the socks up in her mouth, and brought them right back over. "Good girl," I said, and I threw them again.

We played fetch about ten times. I thought it was time to do something else, but Bella nudged the socks closer to me and barked.

"What, Bells, you want to play again?" I asked.

She barked again.

"Or are you saying 'hi'?" I asked. I remembered something Evie told me, about when she taught Bella to sit. She would wait for Bella to sit. Then she'd say the word out loud, in English and in French (Evie speaks TWO languages), and give Bella a treat.

Bella barked a third time. "Say hi," I said. I didn't have a treat to give her, so I threw the socks for her again as a reward. She went off to retrieve them.

When she brought them back, I said, "Say hi," so she'd bark again. But this time, Bella curled up next to me. "Oh, little Bella Malty Maltese malted malteser, you're tired, aren't you?" I got up quickly just to get my notebook, and then I sat right back down next to her.

Someone knocked on the door—there's a sign that says: *This is Stella's Room. If You Are Not Stella Then Please Knock.*

"Who is it?" I asked.

"It's Grandma," Grandma said.

"Come in."

"How's it going in here?" she asked, stepping inside.

"It's great," I said. "Bella's keeping me company while I work on my book. You know, it's helpful having a puppy with me while I write."

"Perhaps this will be your best book yet, with that sweet little thing next to you for company and inspiration," Grandma said.

Even though I hadn't written much of my new book yet, I was pretty sure Grandma was right about that.

CHAPTER 3

To and From

From: Hugh King (HKing@hughdesignit.com)
To: Elaine Batts (elaine@battsconfections.com)
Subject: This is for Stella from Evie

Dear Mrs. Batts,
I don't have my own e-mail so my dad is typing this for me from his account. Can you give this to Stella to read? Stella doesn't have her own e-mail either, so that's why I'm writing to you. Thank you.

Sincerely, Evie King (Stella's friend)

Dear Stella,

I'm testing to see if you get this. We are leaving for the airport to go to London in an hour. My dad says it'll be too much money to call you from there, but I can use his e-mail to say hi and check on Bella. Hi! How is Bella? Did you get this e-mail?
Your friend, Evie

From: Elaine Batts (elaine@battsconfections.com)
To: Hugh King (HKing@hughdesignit.com)
Subject: This is for Evie from Stella

Dear Mr. King,
This is Stella Batts. (Actually, it's my grandma

typing for me, on my mom's e-mail account.)
I hope you have a good trip and I hope you can give this to Evie.
Sincerely,
Stella Batts

Dear Evie,
Yes I got your e-mail! It was my very first e-mail!
My mom isn't checking her e-mail as much since she's busy with the baby, so I didn't know you e-mailed me until just now. Grandma told me it is eight hours later in London, which means it's Saturday night there already. Did you land yet? Over here in Somers, we're getting ready for lunch.
Bella is great. We woke up at the exact same time this morning. I opened my eyes and then she opened her eyes, and we went

for a little stroll with my grandma. Now I'm teaching her a new command—at least in English. Maybe you can teach her the French when you get home.

Love, Stella

P.S. The new command is for her to say "hi." Or actually for her to bark when I ask her to say "hi."

From: Hugh King (HKing@hughdesignit.com)
To: Elaine Batts (elaine@battsconfections.com)
Subject: For Stella again

It's really late but I can't sleep because I'm still on California time. Also because it's raining so hard right now. That made me think of something I have to tell you. If there's a storm in Somers while I'm gone, you should let Bella sleep in the bed with you. She's afraid of thunder.

I'm so happy she's with you instead of the kennel!!! There wouldn't be anyone for her to sleep with!!!

Your friend, Evie

From: Elaine Batts (elaine@battsconfections.com)

To: Hugh King (HKing@hughdesignit.com)

Subject: For Evie

Hi Evie,

There wasn't a thunderstorm last night, but Bella slept with me anyway. Except in the morning I couldn't find her! It made me so scared! Then I noticed my shirt was moving across the floor. Bella was caught underneath it! I'm going to try and keep my

room neater from now on.

Love, Stella

P.S. I don't mind cleaning my room for Bella!

P.P.S. How's your old house?

From: Hugh King (HKing@hughdesignit.com)

To: Elaine Batts (elaine@battsconfections.com)

Subject: Another note to Stella

We're staying with my aunt and uncle and cousins, instead of at our old flat, because there's a new family living there now. I'd like to go visit tomorrow. We could stop by for tea or something, and then I could see what my old room looks like with different furniture in it, and make sure they didn't paint over the inside of the cupboard in the kitchen. That's where my mum marked my height on the first day of school each year. But Mum says we can't visit. I hope she changes her mind. I don't see the harm in it, do you? How is Bella? I miss her so much! I miss you, too!

Your friend,

Evie

From: Elaine Batts (elaine@battsconfections.com)

To: Hugh King (HKing@hughdesignit.com)

Subject: A note for Evie, and a picture

1 Attachment

Dear Evie,

That's too bad about your old flat, but cool about your cousins! I don't have any cousins. Not yet at least. When my Aunt Laura gets married, then I'll get a cousin, because Aunt Laura's husband-to-be has a daughter. But that's not until next month.

But I'll tell you what's happening right now. I'm waiting for my dad to come home and then he's going to take me to the dog run by the reservoir. I've always wanted to go. I've just never had a dog to go with before. When you get home, I'll tell you all about it.

Love,

Stella

P.S. The attachment is a picture of Bella and me that we took on the computer.

P.P.S. Does flat mean apartment?

P.P.P.S. Bella says "ruff!" You know what that means.

CHAPTER 4

If the Shoe Fits

Sunday morning, Mom shook me awake. "Mmm," I groaned. "What time is it?"

"Almost seven," she said.

"In the *morning*? But Mom, it's a weekend."

"The dog needs to go out," she said. "Don't you hear her barking?"

"Mmm," I said, burrowing under the covers. "I thought it was part of my dream."

"Come on, Stel. Up and at 'em."

"Can't you take her, just this once? You're

already awake."

Mom shook her head.

"What about Dad?" I asked. "Is he up?"

"He's getting ready to go to the store, and besides, Stel, Bella is *your* responsibility. Hurry now. I don't want her having an accident."

"Okay, fine," I said. I got out of my warm cozy bed. Bella was waiting for me by the front door. Mom watched on the stoop as we walked in front of the house. When Bella went to the bathroom, I had to clean it up. I held my nose as I picked it up in a plastic bag, and then I stuck the bag in the garbage cans by the curb. YUCK! Bella trotted beside me on her leash, wagging her tail. How could something so cute do something so gross? I guess she's kind of like Marco that way.

When I came back inside, Mom didn't even have to remind me to wash my hands.

But the rest of the morning with Bella was totally fun. First she came back into my bed with me and cuddled (I made sure she was all clean first), then we practiced her sitting and shaking commands (in English and French). I tried to get her to bark "hi" again, but she'd forgotten how to do it.

Still, a baby dog can do a lot more than a baby person. Marco couldn't even walk, and Bella could walk and run and do tricks.

I ate breakfast and Bella ate hers right

beside me (on the floor). When I walked into the living room, Bella followed right behind me. "Look at this," I said to Penny. She was sitting on the floor, even though there's a perfectly good couch against the wall, and two comfy chairs. "Bella knows how to heel."

"Ga!" Penny said.

"What?"

"Goo goo ga," she said. "I don't know the word 'heel.' I'm too little."

"It means Bella doesn't run ahead and she doesn't get too far behind. She stays at my heels. Get it?"

Penny didn't answer.

"Are you coming to the dog run with Daddy and me?" I asked. "He said he would take me as soon as he got home. He just had to do a work errand first."

"Goo," she said, shaking her head no.

"Why are you talking like that?"

"Shrinky-dinky."

"What?"

"I made an invention," she said, speaking super fast. "It's called a shrinkenator. Now I can go back and be a baby again. I need bottles and I can't walk and I can't learn new words and I can't answer any more questions! Goo goo ga ga ga!"

"Penny?" Mom called. "Stella?" She walked into the room, and Bella trotted over toward her. "What do you want?" Mom asked Bella.

"She thought you wanted her," I said. "You said 'Stella,' and that's pretty close to 'Bella.' She's smart, huh?"

"Mmm hmm," Mom said. She didn't bend down to pet Bella, so I did it for her. "What's going on with you, Pen?" Mom asked.

"Ga," Penny said.

"Sorry, I didn't catch that."

"Ga," Penny repeated.

"She's trying to be a baby," I said. "That's why she's talking that way."

"Penny, you're five years old. Use your words, please," Mom said.

"But you love babies best!" Penny said.

"That's not true."

"Okay, not all babies. But Marco—you love that baby better than me!"

"That's just not true," Mom said. "I love you both the same."

"I love you all the way to the sky," Penny said. "That's really far."

"It certainly is far," Mom said. "I love you even farther than that—so far you can't even measure it."

"Is that farther than you love Marco?"

"Oh, Penny," Mom said, sighing. "Come here."

Mom sank into one of the comfy chairs and held her arms out. Penny climbed into them. Mom petted Penny's head, just the way I pet Bella's. But then Grandma came in with Marco in her arms. He was making eensy weensy cries. "Elaine, I think this little guy is hungry again."

I thought so too, because of Marco's little cries. When Mom doesn't feed him right away, he gets louder and louder.

"Pen, I'm going to need you to get up now," Mom told her. "Time to get dressed for the day, okay?"

"I'm staying in my pj's," Penny said.

"No," Mom said as she gently pushed

Penny off to the side and reached out for Marco. "It's time to get ready for the day."

"But Marco gets to stay in his pj's! He even gets the footie kind! It's not fair!"

Penny usually copies me. Now she wanted to copy Marco. Why couldn't she just be herself?

"How about a compromise?" Mom asked. "You can stay in your pajamas while you walk the dog with Stella—as long as you put some shoes on."

"I'm taking her out when Dad comes home," I reminded Mom. "We're going to the dog park."

"And I'm too little to walk the dog," Penny cried.

"She's sniffing around quite a bit," Mom said. "I don't think you should wait."

Bella was sniffing the edge of the couch.

She went over to Grandma and started sniffing her shoe. "That's just what she does when she's exploring," I said. But right then Bella squatted down—she's so tiny that she doesn't have far to squat—and peed right there on the rug next to Grandma.

"I told you she needed to go out, Stella," Mom said. "Bad dog! Bad, bad dog!"

"Don't yell at her," I said.

"She's just a puppy, Elaine," Grandma added. "And she's in a strange house. It's understandable that she had an accident."

Mom took a deep breath. "Stella," she said, "you need to clean that up and take her out."

Now that Bella had gone to the bathroom, I was pretty sure she didn't have to go out, but I didn't say that to Mom.

Grandma got paper towels and some

cleaning spray from the kitchen. She squirted the spray and I pressed a bunch of paper towels into the carpet to soak it all up. After, you could still see the spot. I hoped it would dry up and disappear. I didn't want Mom to stay mad at Bella—or at me.

Dad's car pulled into the driveway right then. I scooped Bella up and ran to the front door. Her leash was on the table where we drop the mail, so I grabbed it and put on my shoes—I mean Evie's shoes, the ones with the eensy weensy heels I'd traded her for.

Dad pushed open the door, his cell phone pressed to his ear. "All right. Great. I'll see you in a few," he said.

"Who will you see in a few?" I asked after he'd pressed the button to hang up. "You're still taking us to the dog run, right?"

"Right. Just have to get something at the store—the shipment I was waiting for just arrived."

"Cool," I said. I snapped Bella's leash onto her collar. "Let's go right now!"

CHAPTER 5

Who's in Charge?

Dad pulled the car out of the driveway and we were on our way. I held Bella in my arms all the way to Batts Confections. She was too little for her own seat belt.

"Come on, Bella Marshmallow," I said when we pulled in to the parking lot. "I'm going to show you Batts Confections!"

"Hold on, Stel," Dad said. "Somers city law says no animals in a store where food is sold. Leave her here and I'll crack the window."

"But I promised Evie I'd take care of Bella," I said. "I can't leave her alone in the car. How about if you go in the store and I stand outside?" He didn't answer for a second. "Mom had me do the same thing at home," I added quickly. "She watched me through the window while I walked Bella. This is even safer, because I don't have to walk anywhere at all."

"All right," Dad said. "If you stay right outside where I can see you, and you don't talk to anyone you don't know."

We walked up to the store, and Dad went inside. Stuart knocked on the window from the inside and waved to Bella and me.

"Stella, is that you?" a voice from behind me asked.

I turned around and guess who was there? Mrs. Finkel! I'd never seen a teacher on a weekend before.

Mrs. Finkel didn't look the way she usually did. Instead of a blouse and skirt, she was wearing a navy blue T-shirt and jeans. There was a boy next to her, younger than Penny and me, but definitely older than Marco. "Evan, this is Stella," Mrs. Finkel told him. "She's one of my students. Stella, this is my son, Evan."

Her son? I didn't know she had a kid. I didn't know a lot of things about her, like:

 Did she have more than one kid?

2. Did she have a best friend?

3. Did she have a husband?

 If she did have a husband, what was his name? (Her first name is Dara. I know because I've heard other teachers say it.)

5. What color house did they live in?

Mrs. Finkel had a whole life outside of our class. Like she made grocery lists and had a favorite song and took out the garbage.

"Is that your dog?" Evan asked me.

"Uh . . . yeah, it is," I said. It wasn't really a

lie, since Bella was mine for the weekend, plus two more days.

"I have a dog, too," Evan said.

Mrs. Finkel had a kid and a dog?

"What kind of dog?" I asked.

"A miniature schnauzer," Evan said.

"I don't know that kind."

"There's one in the window at Man's Best Friend."

"We should get going, Ev," Mrs. Finkel said. "We have to pick up Shadow."

"Who's Shadow?" I asked.

"My dog," Evan said.

"You're buying him today?"

"No, he was just in for a grooming."

"It was good to see you, Stella," Mrs. Finkel said. "I'll see you at school tomorrow."

We said good-bye. I watched them walk down the sidewalk and turn the corner.

Right past the corner is Man's Best Friend. Then I looked back at the window of Batts Confections. I didn't see Dad, but I saw Claire. She works at the store. She smiled and pushed open the door. "Hello, Miss Batts," she said. "Your dad's downstairs, but I told him I'd watch you through the window until he came back up. Need anything? Some fudge maybe?"

"No thanks," I said. "Can you just tell him Bella and I are going to go to Man's Best Friend? We'll be right back."

"Are you allowed to go there alone?"

"My teacher's there right now, so I wouldn't be there alone." Mrs. Finkel was in charge of me all day long at school, so I figured she could be in charge of me at the pet store. "Can you tell him?"

"Sure," Claire said.

"Thanks. Come on, Bells," I said, pulling on Bella's leash. We skipped down the sidewalk—well, I skipped and Bella jogged beside me. "Look, the window dogs!" I told her. "Wave hello." I picked her up and shook her paw for her.

Mrs. Finkel came back outside with Evan—and Shadow. Right away, the dogs started sniffing each other. Mrs. Finkel glanced around. "You're here alone?" she asked me.

I didn't tell her what I'd said to Claire— that I was there with *her*, so it was okay.

Instead I said, "My dad's at the store."

"You should head back there, then," she said.

Mrs. Finkel was in charge of me, so I guess I had to listen to her. Even though she was a teacher, and I don't think teachers usually get to be in charge on the weekends.

Just then I heard my name in the loudest, screamiest voice ever: "STELLA!"

It was Dad's voice.

"STELLA!" called another voice. Stuart, this time.

Then they shouted together: "STELLAAAAAAAA!"

"I'M COMING!" I shouted back. I scooped Bella up and started running. Evie's shoes almost slipped off my feet with each step. I had to curl my toes to try and keep them on.

I rounded the corner. But then something happened. I didn't curl my toes tight enough and my heel came all the way out of my right shoe. Bella's leash got caught under my foot. Then Bella and I were both headed straight toward the ground.

I was going to land on Bella! No, I couldn't let that happen! She was my responsibility! I bent my knees and stuck out the arm that wasn't holding her. Whack, my knees and then my wrist hit the ground. Bella was safe. That was a close one.

But OWWWWWW! My knees! My

wrist! Dad ran up to me. "I think I broke something," I told him.

Usually when I'm hurt, Dad gathers me up in his arms. He blows on my cuts and scrapes to make them feel better.

But not this time.

"Stella Rae Batts," he said.

Uh-oh. Dad was using my whole name. I was in big trouble. But the different parts of me were stinging so much that I didn't even care.

"Those knees look pretty scraped up," Stuart said. "How's your wrist? Can you bend it?"

I bent it back and forth. "Thatta girl," Stuart said. He turned to Dad. "The first-aid kit's inside."

"All right. Let's head in," Dad said.

"What about Bella?" I asked.

"She'll have to wait out here," he said sternly. He reminded me of Mom right then, like someone who didn't care about Bella. "I'll tie her leash to the meter."

"No," I started. I've seen other people tie up their dogs, and I've always felt sorry for them, having to wait all alone.

"If you hadn't wandered off, this wouldn't have happened," Dad said. "Now either let me tie her, or you can do it yourself."

I knew he meant business. I limped over to the parking meter right outside the store, and tied the leash tight as I could. Then I double-knotted it, just in case.

The first-aid kit was behind the register. Stuart went to get it. I was crying hard by then, partly because Dad was mad at me and partly because my knees and my wrist were hurting. A LOT.

Claire brought over a chocolate Band-Aid and held it out toward me, but Dad shook his head no. "You're eight years old, Stella," he said. "That means you're old enough to know you're not allowed to go off on your own."

"I didn't go off on my own," I wailed. "Mrs. Finkel was there, and Bella wanted to see the window dogs, and I'm in charge of taking care of her."

"And I'm in charge of YOU," Dad said. "I shouldn't have left you alone but you shouldn't have left."

"It's my fault," Claire said. "She said she was allowed, and . . ."

"No, it's not your fault," Dad told her. "Stella knew better."

Stuart came back with bandages and that spray stuff to put on cuts. It's supposed to make them better, but really it just makes them sting worse. I squeezed my eyes shut and gritted my teeth.

A bell rang as someone pushed the front door open. "Did someone have a dog tied up out there?" a lady called out.

I opened my eyes as Dad said, "Yes, we did." The lady was standing in the doorway. Beyond her, I could see the parking meter. The meter without Bella attached to it.

"The leash came loose and I didn't catch her in time," the lady said. She lifted her arm up and pointed to the left. "She went that way."

Bella was gone!!!

Oh no oh no oh no oh no oh no oh no oh no oh no oh no oh no oh no!!!

CHAPTER 6

Lost

I raced out the door. I didn't even feel the cuts stinging anymore. I could only feel my heart thumping harder than it had ever thumped before.

First Dad and I ran left, the direction the lady had pointed. No Bella. Then we doubled back and went right, but there was no sign of her that way, either. Stuart and Claire promised to keep an eye out in the shopping center. Dad and I got into the car to drive around and look some more.

I wiped my face with my hands and swallowed the big lump in my throat. "We'll find her, right?" I asked Dad, as he turned the key to start the car.

"We'll certainly try, darling," he said.

Usually parents tell their kids that everything will be okay. So I knew that this time, it really might not be.

We drove down practically every street in all of Somers. I looked out the window and called, "Bella! Bella!" as we went.

We turned the corner on Monticello Road. Down the street, I could see someone waving. Dad slowed the car to a stop and Lucy from my class came running up to my window. "Stella! I knew it was you! I recognized your dad's car!"

I wished she hadn't seen me. I wanted to roll up my window and have us drive down the next street. What if Bella was one block over right now? And we missed her because I'd been talking to Lucy?

Lucy was with her sister, Ann. Ann is already a teenager, and she babysits sometimes. "Come on, Luce," Ann said, impatiently. "I have to call Oliver back."

"Wait a sec," Lucy told her. "What's wrong?" she asked me.

"Nothing," I said.

"It's not nothing. You were crying. I can tell because there are dried-up tears on your face."

Dad twisted around in his seat. "We're looking for Evie's dog," he said. "Can you keep an eye out for a little white Maltese?"

"Bella's missing?" Lucy asked. "What

happened? I thought Evie was going to England."

I just shook my head. I couldn't talk anymore.

But Dad filled her in: "Evie is in England. We were watching Bella for her, and she got away."

"Have you been to the pound?" Lucy asked. "In the movies, that's where people always bring lost dogs."

In the movies, the dogs at the pound are always MISERABLE.

"We're hoping someone found her and is keeping her safe until we get there," Dad said.

"I'll make up some lost dog signs," Lucy said. "Just send me a picture."

"That's a very kind offer, Lucy," Dad said.

"We REALLY have to go," Ann told Lucy, pulling on her arm.

"Okay," Lucy said and Dad pulled the car away. When we stopped at the stop sign at the end of the street, he turned to look at me. "I think it's time for us to go home, too."

"But we haven't found Bella yet!"

"I know, and I'm sorry. We can go out looking again a little bit later, but I think we should check in on everyone at home. Grandma must be about ready to leave and go back to her own house. Don't you want to say good-bye to her?"

"You don't think we'll ever find Bella, do you?" I asked.

"Oh, darling," Dad said.

He was calling me "darling," which meant he wasn't mad at me anymore for walking out of his sight. And he didn't answer the question, which meant he didn't think we'd find Bella.

"Here," he said. "This is the package I

went back to the store for—mini brownies and cupcakes. Chocolate may not cure heartache, but it helps. What would you say to a treat? You must be hungry, since you didn't even have lunch."

He was trying to distract me. That's his trick whenever Penny and I are upset about something. But Penny gets upset about little things, like when her stuffed animal, Belinda, went missing.

Bella was a real-live dog. Distraction wasn't going to work on me. "I don't want any treat right now," I told him.

"Maybe later," he said.

"Maybe never," I answered back.

I'd give up chocolate for the rest of my entire life, if only we could find Bella.

I kept the window open and looked for Bella as we drove home, but we didn't see her. Grandma had her suitcases by the front door, and she pulled me into the tightest hug when Dad told her what happened.

"Please don't leave," I said. "I need you to take me out to look for Bella again."

"I'm sorry, sweetheart," Grandma said. "I've got to get back to Grandpa. But I'll keep an eye out for Bella as I'm driving through town to the highway."

The highway! Bella wouldn't go there, would she? What if she did and she got hit by a speeding car?

"This is an emergency!" I said. "We have to call the police!"

Dad shook his head. "You know, Stel, I don't think this is the kind of emergency the police respond to."

"But Bella is missing! She could be headed toward the highway right now!"

"I know, darling," he said. "But the police are more for people emergencies—not dog ones."

Grandma gave me another big hug. "When I see you at Aunt Laura's wedding

next month, you can tell me all about how you found Bella," she told me. Then she hugged everyone else good-bye.

She left, and I said I wanted to go to my room. Mom said she wanted me to sit with her. Dad took Marco from her arms, and

Mom and I cuddled up on the couch in the living room. "Oh, Stella, my poor baby," she said.

"*She's* your baby now?" Penny asked. "That's no fair! You won't let me be a baby, and Stella's even older than I am!"

"Stella is my first baby," Mom said. "You're my middle baby, and Marco is my littlest baby."

Penny folded her arms across her chest. She made a *humph* noise, and then settled down in the chair across from us.

"I don't like being in here when Bella's out there," I told Mom.

"You know," Mom said, "I've read that if ever someone goes missing, you're supposed to stay put. That way, when they're trying to make their way back to you, they know where to find you. Maybe the place you're supposed to be is right here, because that's what Bella would expect of you."

"But that rule is for people, and Bella's a dog."

"She's a smart dog."

That was true. Bella understood different languages, and heeled without you even having to tell her. But even a smart dog could get into trouble when she was out in the world, all alone.

"You're probably glad that she's gone," I told Mom. "She's not shedding on the furniture, or sniffing anything, or having an accident, or going anywhere near Marco!"

"I'm not a pet person, Stella," Mom said. "But I'm very sad that this happened. I'd rather have that dog living with us all weekend—I'd rather have that dog living with us all month— than have to see you so upset."

"I can't be in charge of a dog for a month," I told her. "I can't be in charge of a dog at all."

"Oh, Stel."

"It's all my fault. If Bella had just gone to the kennel, like Mrs. King had planned, she wouldn't be lost right now. People shouldn't trust me with anything."

"Of course, people should trust you," Mom said. "I trust you with lots of things— like with your brother. He's just a baby, but I know you're grown up enough to hold him and feed him, even to change his diaper."

"But not the gross ones," I said.

"He's clean now," she said. "Maybe you'd feel better if you held him. Do you want me to have Dad bring him back in? Sometimes holding a baby makes a person feel better."

"Holding Marco won't make me feel better," I said.

"Maybe if you hold *me* you'll feel better," Penny told me. She stood up from the chair and moved toward us on the couch.

"No thanks," I said. "I don't want to hold anyone."

"Can you hold me, Mommy?" Penny asked.

"In a little while, honey," Mom told her. "I need to be with Stella right now."

"First you can't be with me because you're with Marco, then you can't be with me because you're with Stella! It's not fair!"

"Penny!" Mom said. "I'm Stella's and Marco's mommy, too. Sometimes your brother and sister need me."

"But I need you."

"Sometimes they need me more than you do."

"It's okay," I said. "You can be with Penny.

I want to be alone."

Penny leaped onto Mom the instant I stood up. "Come get me if you need me," Mom said.

I walked down the hall to my room and pushed open the door. On the other side— DISASTER!

CHAPTER 7

More Bad News

It looked like a tornado had hit my room.

All the blankets that were supposed to be on the bed were on the floor. So were my stuffed animals and my books and the deck of cards to play Spit. The cards were out of the package and spread out like they'd been dropped like confetti. My dresser drawers were all open, the clothes spilling out.

Maybe I'm not the neatest girl in the world. And maybe I don't make my bed perfectly every morning. And maybe sometimes I forget to put my clothes in the hamper at the end of the day.

But this was messier than my room had ever been.

For a second I was speechless. And then the tears came all over again, hot as fudge straight out of the oven. I shouted as loud as I could: "MOM! DAD! COME QUICK!"

Mom came racing in. Dad was right behind her, with Marco in his arms.

I didn't even need to tell them what was wrong. They knew just by looking.

They also knew who did it.

"Penny!" Dad said sharply, which made Marco start to cry a little bit. Well, that made two of us. Dad jiggled him up and down.

"Penny!" Mom repeated, just as sharply.

Penny was nowhere in sight. It was the

first time in days she hadn't been at Mom's side.

I was still in the doorway, but now I stepped farther into the room. Something cracked under my foot. My little clay turtle. "Oh no, it's broken," I said, holding out the pieces toward Mom and Dad.

My best friend Willa and I had made twin turtles. We let the clay dry instead of smashing it up and putting it back in the can. Before she moved to Pennsylvania, I gave  Willa mine. Then she gave me hers. That way we could remember each other. But now it was ruined.

"I'm going to find your sister," Mom said.

When Mom came back, she was dragging Penny by the hand. "Penelope Jane," Dad said, in a voice I recognized—his angry voice. "Your sister's room is a mess."

Penny nodded, and babbled like a baby.

"Why did you do this?" Mom asked. "And I want to hear your words, Penny. No baby talk."

"I didn't know any better."

"That's just not true," Mom said. "You know the difference between right and wrong. I know you're having a hard time adjusting to life with a new baby, but you can't make a mess just because you're upset. Now, you're going to clean up this up."

"I don't know how to clean up. I'm too little."

Mom shook her head. "If you're big enough to make a mess in your sister's room, you are big enough to clean it up."

"Mom and I trust you to be careful

around things that belong to other people," Dad added.

Careful around things that belong to other people. I bet that meant dogs, too.

"Does that mean I'm allowed to mess up stuff in my own room?" Penny asked.

"I'd prefer it if you didn't," Mom told her. "But you can do whatever you want to do in your own room."

"You owe Stella an apology," Dad added.

"Sorry," Penny whispered.

"Penny's going to help you clean up now, Stel. Right Penny?" Mom asked.

"Uh huh," she said, nodding. "And you too, Mommy?"

"Yes, I'll help you too. We'll get this back in order, Stella. Don't you worry."

"I wasn't worried about my room being in order," I said. "I'm only worried about Bella."

"I know, darling, I know," Dad said. But then Marco started crying harder, and Dad left the room to get him settled down. Mom pulled the sheets back onto my bed, and then Penny pulled up the blanket, way messier than usual. "Not so fast," Mom told her. "You have to tuck the corners of the sheet in first."

"You know what's a good invention?" Penny asked. "Sleeping bags! If we just put a sleeping bag on the mattress instead of sheets and covers, it would be easier to make the bed every day."

I agreed with her, but I didn't say anything. I was just thinking about Bella. Where was she, right now? What if we didn't find her before nighttime? Where would she be sleeping, if she wasn't in my warm cozy bed with me? Would she be shivering on the street all alone? Or was she with another family? Were they being nice to her, and were they trying to find her real home?

They wouldn't keep her for themselves, would they? That'd be kidnapping! Or at least dognapping.

"I don't think that's a good idea," Mom told Penny. "But I'll make the bed for you. Why don't you tackle the stuff on the floor? You too, Stel."

So that's what we did. Penny picked up the clothes and folded them back up. She didn't do such a good job, though. But that wasn't her acting like a baby. She's NEVER been good at folding clothes.

I started picking up the stuff that belonged on my desk, like my Disneyland mug that I used as a pencil holder, all the pencils that went inside it, my Dad's old gym membership card that looks like a credit card, and my new *Superstar Sam* notebook, where I keep my list of story ideas.

Superstar Sam is my favorite TV show—Willa's, too. It's about a girl named Sam who's a gymnast. If I were famous like Sam, I'd have so many bodyguards around, they would've been there to watch Bella when I went inside to get my cuts cleaned up. Of course, if I were Sam, I'd be so well coordinated, I never would've tripped in the first place.

The phone started ringing and didn't stop. "I'll be back in a minute," Mom said.

Penny scampered out the door after Mom. I turned back to my desk. I'd actually made things look neater than they did *before* Penny messed it all up.

But wait! What about MY books? The books I wrote myself? I have four of them so far—this book you're reading is book number five. What if Penny had gone through my top drawer and ruined them too?

My heart went THUMP THUMP THUMP. My books are my most special things. That's why they're in the top drawer, piled up so neat. Neater than I keep anything else.

At least that's the way they're supposed to be.

I could barely breathe as I pulled open the drawer.

And then I saw them. My books, stacked up the way they always were. Safe and sound.

Safe and sound. Suddenly I was thinking about Bella again. My eyes got hot, like I'd been sucking on a spicy mint—the kind that I don't like because it tastes too much like mouthwash.

I closed my desk drawer. I didn't want to look at my books anymore.

"Stella!" Mom called.

"Yeah?"

Mom walked back into my room. The phone was in her hands and she held it out toward me. "It's for you. It's Lucy."

I didn't want to talk to anyone, but I was sure Lucy had heard Mom call my name, and heard me answer, so I took the phone.

"Hello?" I said.

"Hi, Stella," Lucy said. "Have you found Bella yet?"

"No, not yet," I said.

"Okay, good," Lucy said. "Well, not good. It'd be good if you found her, of course. But it's okay because I have lots—"

Beep went the call waiting. I checked the screen: caller unknown.

"I have to go," I said. "Someone else is calling and it's probably for my mom or dad."

"I have lots of ideas for finding her, that's what I was going to say," Lucy said. "Call me back."

Beep! the call waiting went again.

"Bye," I said. I clicked over. "Hello?"

"Hello, Stella?" a voice said—a voice with an accent. "Stella, is that you?"

Oh no! It was Evie!

CHAPTER 8

Awkward

This is how the phone call went; I'll write it out like a play:

Evie: Hi! How are you?

Me: You're home? What are you doing home?

Evie: No, no, I'm still in London.

Me: Who is that in the background? Your cousins?

Evie: Nope, it's Sara and Tesa. I'm at their house right now. My cousins are older, so they're not so fun to play with. It's super late here, but we're trying to stay awake the whole night so we get more time together.

Me: If you're calling from England, it's probably very expensive.

Evie: That's okay. Their parents don't mind. I wanted to know how Bella was. Can you put her on the phone?

Me: She can't talk.

Evie: Didn't you teach her to bark when you say hi?

Me: She's not so good at it yet.

Evie: But she could hear my voice at least, and I could hear her breathing. Please?

(This is when I pretended to put the phone to Bella's ear. Since Evie couldn't see anything through the phone, she wouldn't know it was really still just me.)

Me: Okay, you can talk to her.

Evie: Hi, Bella! Hi, Bellzy-blue!

Sara and Tesa: Hi!!!!

Evie: Did you hear that, Bella? My friends are saying hi to you. I've told them all about your tricks. Can you sit, Bella? Sit. Is she sitting, Stella?

Me: Uh, yeah. And she's . . . uh . . . she's wagging her tail.

Evie: Oh, I miss her so much. I want to know everything that's going on. What did you guys do today?

Me: What's that? I'm starting to not be able to hear you so well. It must be because you're really far away. I'll talk to you when you get home!

Click.

In the morning, Mom put out bowls of cereal for breakfast.

Penny opened her mouth like a bird, for Mom to feed her. "No, no, Pen," Mom said, handing her the spoon. "You do it yourself."

"Wah," Penny said, but she dipped the spoon into the bowl and lifted it up to her mouth, all on her own.

Mom turned to me. "I know you're upset about Bella, but you still have to eat."

"That's not it," I said. "I mean, that's only partly it." I paused. Mom nodded at me to keep going. "The other part is that I lied to Evie last night."

"Was this a dream you had?"

"No, this was real life. She called and asked me to put Bella on the phone, but, of course, I couldn't." I could feel my eyes starting to get wet again. "Am I in trouble now?"

"Dad and I want you to tell the truth, even when it's the hard thing to do," Mom started.

Oh no, I *was* in trouble. I probably deserved to be.

"But right now Evie's five thousand miles away, so there's nothing she can do for Bella. I think you did the right thing this time, letting her enjoy her time in London. Hopefully when she's back, Bella will be too."

"It's already Monday. Evie's coming home tomorrow," I reminded Mom.

"I know," Mom said. "So Bella has the whole day to be found."

"Can I have more juice?" Penny asked.

"What do you say?"

"*Please* can I have more juice," Penny repeated.

"Of course," Mom said. She poured Penny a drink and told us to eat up—"you too, Stella"—because Mrs. Benson would be picking us up soon.

I took a bite of cereal—three Cheerios floating in a spoon of milk—but my stomach felt weird and swirly, like someone was mixing up a batch of fudge inside of it. That made it hard to swallow like normal.

"I shouldn't go to school," I said. "I should be out looking for Bella."

"School is your job," Mom said. "You can't miss it. And maybe being there will be good for you—get your mind off of it."

"My mind will still be on it," I said. "It was all I was thinking about last night. I couldn't even sleep because I was thinking so much about Bella."

"Just do your best today, Stel, okay?"

"If Marco went missing, you'd be out looking for him. Dad too. You wouldn't worry about your jobs."

"A dog is a little different than a baby," Mom said. "But Marco and I will take a drive this morning and look for her, okay?"

Mrs. Benson beeped her horn a few minutes later. Penny and I were in the front hall, with our shoes on our feet and our backpacks on our shoulders. Dad had already left for the store. Mom stood at the door with

Marco in her arms.

Penny was right. It was better to be a baby. Marco wasn't worried about anything because he didn't know how to worry. If I was a baby, I wouldn't be worried, either. I wouldn't have been watching Bella, and I wouldn't have lost her. And then Lucy wouldn't have seen me riding around in Dad's car, looking for the dog. She wouldn't have called me about it last night, and she wouldn't be waiting for me at school to talk about it some more. If I were a baby, I could stay home all day with Mom.

I clicked my heels together three times, the way I do when I really want something to happen, and I wished there really were such a thing as a shrinkenator. Then I could go backward and not have to worry about all the things that can go wrong when you're eight.

CHAPTER 9

At School and After That

Of course, my wish didn't work, so I had to ride in Mrs. Benson's car, to Somers Elementary School.

Sometimes Mrs. Benson gets us to school late. Being late is usually NOT one of my favorite things. But today I didn't mind at all. I walked into my classroom just as Mrs. Finkel was clapping her hands. That meant it was time for everyone to be sitting at their desks, and for our first lesson of the day to begin.

Lucy caught my eye and mouthed, "Did you find her?" I pretended not to know what she was saying. It was bad enough that I'd lost Bella! I didn't want to have to talk about it! Instead, I concentrated on Mrs. Finkel's lessons.

But soon it would be snack time. Maybe I'd go to the bathroom for the first half of snack, when we're allowed to stand up and stretch and talk to each other. I wouldn't come back until after the halfway point, when we have to be back at our own desks.

Oh no, but what about lunch? We're allowed to talk to each other the whole entire period.

I'd have to think of another plan.

I could pretend to be sick and get to go home early. That happened once before, and Mom wasn't mad at all. Except I had a feeling she'd be mad if I did it a second time. She'd already told me it was my job to be in school.

When Mrs. Finkel clapped her hands to signal the beginning of snack, I was all set to ask to go to the bathroom. But before I could, Lucy raced up to my desk. "Did you find her?" she asked out loud.

"Find who?" Joshua practically shouted, butting in as usual.

"Inside voice, Joshua," Mrs. Finkel said.

"It's none of your beeswax," Lucy said, her voice just a little above a whisper.

Oh good, I thought.

"But if she's still lost we need more people looking so I'll tell you. Evie's dog. Stella was watching her and she got away."

"Ooh, Stella, you lost Evie's dog!" Joshua cried. "That's bad. That's really, REALLY bad."

"Joshua!" Mrs. Finkel said.

"Sorry," he said, in a regular talky voice. But it was too late. Everyone had heard, and they were all looking at me. Talisa came

to my side. "Maybe Stella found her already," she told Joshua. "Did you ever think of that?"

"Did you find her?" Joshua asked.

"No," I said. I looked straight down at my desk as I said it.

"I'm sorry," Arielle said quietly. If marshmallow fluff had a voice, it would sound just like Arielle, comfy and soft.

Joshua's voice is exactly the opposite. "Evie's going to be even MORE sorry," he said.

I knew it was true.

"But it's okay," Lucy said. "I have the perfect plan to get her back, and everyone can help. Hold on, I'll show you."

She went back to her desk and came right back over, carrying a pile of paper as thick as the width of a Batts Confections candy bar. The top sheet said:

DOG MISSING!!!!!!!!!!!!!!!!!!!

Her name is Bella. If you find her before Tuesday, call Stella Batts. If you find her after Tuesday, call Evie King. Or you can just call me anytime. My name is Lucy Anderson.

In the center, there was a big picture of Bella sitting in the grass. Our phone numbers were listed at the bottom of the page.

By then, there were more kids gathered around my desk, all waiting to hear about Lucy's plan. "The sheets are all the same?" Talisa asked her.

"Yup," said Lucy. "I printed out three hundred copies, so Stella can have some, and you can have some. Anyone who wants some can have some. Then we'll put them up around town. The more people putting up signs, the better chance we have to find her. Even you can have some, Joshua." Then she turned to me. "What do you think?"

"Where'd you get the picture of Bella?"

As secretly as I could, I clicked my heels together three times: *Please not from Evie. I don't want her to know I'm the worst dogsitter ever. Please, let Bella be found before Evie gets home, and then she'll NEVER have to know.*

"Oh, it's not really Bella," Lucy said. "I just

used a picture of a Maltese puppy that I found on the Internet. It looks a lot like her, right?"

"It sure does," Joshua said.

"How do you know what Bella looks like?" I asked.

"I've seen Evie walking her, duh!" he said. "But she kept her on a leash so she didn't get away."

I'd kept Bella on her leash, too. She ran off with her leash attached!

"How about twenty sheets each?" Lucy asked.

"Knock knock," Talisa said. Talisa tells knock-knock jokes whenever she gets a chance.

"Who's there?" Lucy asked.

"Ida."

"Ida who?

"Ida want twenty sheets—I want thirty!"

Talisa said. "Get it, I *don't* want twenty. I want even more."

"I get it," Lucy said. "That's great!"

Mrs. Finkel clapped her hands, which meant it was time to go back to our own desks and eat our snacks.

"But Mrs. F., can I please just hand out these flyers?" Lucy asked. "Stella was watching Evie's dog and now she's missing."

"The dog I saw you with?" Mrs. Finkel asked.

I nodded. If only I'd listened to Mrs. Finkel when I saw her, and gone back to the store, Bella would be safe and sound right now!

"I thought that was your dog," she said.

"She was just mine for the weekend," I said super softly.

Mrs. Finkel paused for a second. She

was probably thinking what a bad dogsitter I was—that she'd never let me watch Shadow! "She had her collar on, right? So someone will find her, and make a call."

"The tags fell off her collar," I said, even softer this time—softer even than Arielle's voice.

"So can I hand out the flyers, Mrs. Finkel?" asked Lucy.

"All right, Lucy," Mrs. Finkel said. "Go ahead."

Everyone already knew about Bella, so I didn't pretend to be sick at lunch. Kids planned what streets they'd be in charge of. You were supposed to put up signs on the telephone poles. If you had extras, you could stick them in people's mailboxes. Lucy gave me a really big pile—at least fifty sheets. I was in charge of my street, Tollridge Court, and also Hilltop Acres, where Evie lives.

Mrs. Benson drove Penny and me home. As we walked across the parking lot to her car, Lucy called out, "Call me if you find her or if you need more flyers!"

It's hard to click your heels together as you're walking, but that's what I did: I wished the reason I'd have to call Lucy was because Bella was found.

Mom was waiting for us when we got home. She gave us cookies and milk as an after-school treat. I think she was trying to make me feel better. But since Bella was still missing, it didn't work.

"Coming in for a landing!" Penny said, as she brought the cookie closer to her mouth. "It's flying!" She took a bite of cookie. "What were you flying with Lucy?" she asked.

"Don't talk with your mouth full," I told her.

Penny opened her mouth to show me all the little bits of chewed-up cookie inside. "I don't have to listen to you," she said. But then she swallowed. "Tell me what you were flying."

"None of your beeswax," I told her.

Penny stuck out her lower lip. "That's not fair," she whined. "Mommy, Stella's being really mean to me."

"What happened?" Mom asked.

"Nothing except she's acting like a baby again," I complained.

"No!" Penny said. "Stella was flying something with Lucy and she won't tell me what it was!"

"That's because we weren't flying

anything."

"Then why did I hear Lucy say so?" Penny asked.

"She didn't say flying. She said flyers—that means signs."

"Signs? Like signs of rain, because it's in the sky? But I didn't see any clouds."

"No," I said.

"Then what?"

"None of your—" I started to say, but Mom gave me a Look. "Missing-dog signs. Lucy asked me to put them up on Tollridge, and also at Hilltop Acres. But Bella runs fast. She's probably far, far away by now."

The spicy mint feeling behind my eyes was back again. "May I be excused now?" I asked Mom.

"Are you sure?" Mom asked. "You didn't finish your snack. Why don't you sit with

Penny and me? When Dad comes back, he can watch Marco and I'll take you around to put up the flyers."

"Can I come with you, Mommy?" Penny asked.

"Of course," Mom said.

"No thanks, I don't want to go," I said. "They won't work anyway. It's not even really Bella in the picture."

"Stella—" Mom started, but then she changed her mind. "All right. You're excused."

I went to my room. A few minutes later, Penny came in WITHOUT knocking.

"You have to knock!" I reminded her.

Penny went back out into the

hall. She knocked on my door. "Don't come in!" I said.

She came back in anyway.

"I said don't come in."

There went Penny's lower lip again, pushed out in a super pout. "It's not fair," she said. She stomped out, and I heard her calling through the hall, "Mo-om!"

When Penny really wants something, she adds syllables onto people's names.

I knew what was coming next: Mom, into my room to tell me I still had to be nice to Penny, no matter how upset I was about Bella. I listened for her footsteps coming down the hall.

And listened.

And listened.

But she didn't come.

It was fine, since I wanted to be alone

anyway.

My notebook was sitting on top of my desk. When I was all finished writing in it, I'd have written FIVE books. So far, I was up to the part in the story just before Bella went missing. I didn't want to write about what happened. I wished I could skip to the end and just write the part when she was found.

What if we never found her? Then the book wouldn't have an ending. Or I guess it would have an ending, but a really sad one.

Who wants to write a book like that? Not me!

Maybe I'd never finish my fifth book.

It was a long time before anyone knocked on my door again. This time I said, "Come in," but it wasn't Penny on the other side. It was Dad, saying he'd made chicken fingers for dinner, just for him and me.

Marco was in the dining room with us, too, but I don't count him, because he was sleeping in his baby swing the whole time. Mom had taken Penny out for burgers at Brody's Grill. "Penny needed some Mom time," Dad told me. "They're working on a project."

"What is it?"

"None of your beeswax," he said with a smile.

"Penny told you I said that?"

"She sure did," Dad said. "But in this case, it's true."

After dinner, I took a bath and got into bed with a book. Someone else's book. I didn't want to think about writing mine, because that would make me sad about Bella. Of course, I was already sad about Bella. Reading a different book didn't change anything. A little while later, Dad came in to say goodnight. Then Mom did too—she was home with Penny by then, but Penny didn't come in with her. "Lights out now," Mom told me. I turned them out, but I couldn't fall asleep.

I don't know what time it was—sometime very, very late. My room was pitch-dark and the whole house was quiet. Except I thought I heard something. I sat up, listening. My heart started to beat a little bit faster.

There it was again.

If someone breaks into your room at night, is it safer to scream and run to your parents, or stay silent and hope they don't find you?

"Stella?" a voice whispered.

Penny's voice. Not scary at all.

"What are you doing in here?" I hissed.

"I'm bringing you Belinda," she said. "I thought you might be lonely, and she could keep you company, since you don't have Bella sleeping with you tonight, and you said you couldn't sleep last night."

"Thanks," I said.

"I'm leaving now so you don't have to be mad at me."

"I'm not mad at you. You can sleep in here with Belinda and me, if you want."

"Really?"

"Really."

"Really REALLY?!!"

"Shhh . . . you'll wake Mom and Dad. Yeah, come in."

Penny lay down and curled up next to me.

I was about to fall asleep when I had that feeling again. The feeling of someone coming closer, closer. It couldn't be Penny, because she was already there next to me. I put an arm around Penny. I'd have to protect her.

"Stella," came the whisper. "Stella, sweetie, wake up."

"Mommy? Is that you?" Penny whispered.

"Pen, what are you doing in here?"

"I'm allowed," Penny said. "Stella said so."

"It's true," I told her. "What are you doing in here?"

"You have a phone call," Mom said.

"I don't want to talk to anyone," I told her.

"I think you're going to want to talk to this person," she said.

CHAPTER 10

Found

"Hello?"

"Is this Stella?" a woman on the other end of the line asked.

"Yes, it is," I said. "Who is this?"

"My name is Harper Ross," the woman said. "And I think I have some good news for you. I found your dog."

All of a sudden it felt like there was a gobstopper stuck in my throat. It was hard to talk and even hard to breathe. "You found her?

How?" I managed to squeak out. "When?"

"She was wandering around near where I live. I figured she belonged to someone else in the apartment complex, but then I saw one of your flyers on our evening walk just now. The picture matched the pup I'd found. White all over except for the little brown spot on her left ear. And then I called her name, Bella, and she started wagging her little tail, like she was so happy I finally knew who she was. I know it's a bit late, but I had to call anyway."

I was glad she called me and not Lucy, even if they were really Lucy's signs that found Bella.

"After all," Harper continued, "I figured no one would mind a late call to hear their dog had been found."

"I don't mind at all," I said. "How do I get her back?"

"We'll pick her up, Stel," Mom said. She'd been right next to me the whole time, listening to our conversation.

"Oh right," I said. "Where do you live?"

"Hilltop Acres," Harper said.

"You live in Hilltop Acres?"

"You know it?" Harper asked, at the same time Penny said, "That's where we put up signs!"

I turned to Penny. "YOU put up signs?"

"Uh huh. Mom and me both did."

"Mom and I," Mom said.

"Stella?" Harper asked. I'd almost forgotten I was holding the phone. "So you know where Hilltop Acres is?"

"That's where Bella lives. Actually, it's where my friend Evie lives, and Bella belongs to Evie. I'm just watching her while the Kings are away."

Mom was right. Bella *was* smart enough to go home. Just no one was there. For someone who didn't like dogs, she sure did know about them.

"I don't think I know the Kings," Harper said. "Maybe because I don't live here, really. My parents do. I'm just visiting them on my college break."

"Do you have a speakerphone?" I asked. "Can you put it on so I can say hi to Bella?"

"Sure thing," Harper said. A second later, she added, "Okay, Stella, you're on."

"Hi, Bella!" I cried.

Ruff, said Bella. That was her saying hi! She remembered the trick I'd taught her, and now she'd be coming home.

Mom took the phone back from me so she could arrange a Bella pickup. I wanted to go too, but Mom said it was too late and I

should go back to sleep.

Back to sleep meant I'd been sleeping before, which I hadn't. And no way I'd be able to fall asleep now, when I knew Bella was on her way home. But there was no arguing with Mom about it. She left and said I'd see her— and Bella—in the morning. I settled back into bed with Penny.

But wait. The dog in Lucy's flyer wasn't really Bella. Which meant she didn't have that brown fudge smudge spot.

Harper said she found a dog with a brown spot. But she also said she found the dog in the flyer. Was it possible there were TWO little Maltese puppies missing who could both bark hi? Maybe Harper Ross had found the other one.

"Penny, are you awake?" I said.

"Mmm," she said, like she was dreaming of something delicious.

"Penny, wake up. Something doesn't make sense. The flyers didn't have a picture of the real Bella, so how did Harper know about her brown spot?"

"I made new ones," Penny muttered. "With the pictures from Daddy's computer, because you said no one would find Bella with the wrong picture. But Mom made me print them out on the back of Lucy's flyers so we didn't waste paper."

"Thanks, Penny," I said. "And you know what—you're a step the word for me."

"Mmm," she said. "Unicorns love ice cream."

Huh? That made even less sense! "What?" I asked.

But she didn't answer. She'd gone back to dreaming.

CHAPTER 11

Reunions

The next thing I knew, it was morning and Penny was shaking me awake. "She's here! She's here!" Sure enough, there in Penny's arms was a squirming little ball of marshmallow puppy fluff, with a fudge smudge on her ear.

Penny handed Bella over. I've never been so excited to see someone (I mean, see some *dog*) ever in my whole entire life.

I didn't want to put Bella down, but I had to, because it was time to get ready for school.

"Maybe I should stay home and watch her until Evie gets home," I told Mom. Her plane was landing at noon.

Mom shook her head. "I'll watch Bella today."

"But you don't even like her. So what if you stop watching her and she runs away again?"

"I'll take good care of her, Stella," Mom said. "I promise."

"Pinky swear?" Penny asked.

"Pinky swear," Mom said with a smile, and the three of us hooked pinkies. Then we all shook hands on it, because that made it even more official.

It was Dad's day to drive the carpool. Penny and I waved good-bye to Mom and Marco—and Bella. We got to Somers Elementary School a few minutes early, which meant I had time to tell the other kids that Bella had been found. Lucy said, "Hooray!" and the other kids cheered. Then Mrs. Finkel started clapping, but not because she was cheering too. It's just what she does when she means: Be quiet.

"What's going on?" she asked.

"Smella—I mean *Stella*—found Evie's dog," Joshua filled her in. "Too bad she lost her in the first place." Of course, he didn't use his inside voice either. Maybe he doesn't even have one.

For once Mrs. Finkel didn't get mad. "Well that's wonderful news, Stella," she said. "Evan will be happy to hear it, too." She smiled and for a second, it was like she was my friend instead of my teacher. But then she got her teacher-ish look back on her face, and the first lesson began.

After that, it was just an ordinary day.

School, then snack, then more school, then lunch. I'm not going to write down all the details. Except that we had a Spit Tournament at recess and I came in second place. Talisa won.

Dad had said we'd head over to Evie's when school was out—she'd definitely be home from the airport by then. But when I got to the flagpole, it was Penny, Zoey, and Mom instead of Dad! Mom was holding Bella's leash!

Penny and Zoey were crunched down, petting Bella. "Don't you have to be home with Marco?" I asked.

"That's what I thought," Penny said from below.

"I felt like being with the girls today," Mom said. "So Dad came home from work early."

Suddenly there was a big crowd around us—a bunch of kids from my class wanting to say hi to Bella. Bella herself looked a little shaky from all the attention. I picked her up so she wouldn't be too scared, and let everyone pet her while she was in my arms. "Tell Evie I'll call her later," Lucy said.

"Don't tell Evie what happened when you talk to her, okay?"

"I won't," Lucy promised.

"I won't either," said Talisa, and Arielle nodded, too.

It was time to get going. Mom had let me use her cell phone on the drive over, so Evie was waiting on the sidewalk for us by the time we got there. "Bella! Hi, Bella!" she called as we climbed out of the car. Bella barked. "Oh my, she really does say hi back!"

Evie took Bella into her arms. I thought I'd be sad about not having a dog anymore, but mostly I was glad to not be in charge anymore. Mrs. King was thanking Mom for taking care of her.

"I hope she wasn't too much trouble," Mrs. King said.

Mom glanced at me. "No," she said. "Not too much."

"She got lost," I admitted.

"I just saw a sign. I rang your house, but no one was home. Mum said not to worry, though, because she'd talked to your mum, and heard Bella was fine."

"Yeah, she is," I agreed.

"So your signs worked. That means you rescued her—again!" Evie said.

"Actually, it was Penny this time," I said.

"Thanks so much, Penny," Evie said.

"And Lucy made up a bunch of signs to help," I added. "She said she'll call you later, so you can thank her, too."

Evie wanted me to stay for a play date, but Mrs. King said no—they'd just gotten home, and there was lots of unpacking to do. "I have the shoes Stella borrowed," Mom said. She pulled out a bag from the front seat and handed them over. The shoes that started it all. I was happy to see them go.

"Yours are still in my suitcase," Evie said. "Want to keep mine until we can trade back?"

"That's all right," I told her.

We said good-bye and the three of us—Mom, Penny, and I—climbed back into the car. Evie stood on the sidewalk with Bella in her arms, waving as we drove away.

"I'm not ready to let this girls' day end so fast," Mom said. "So where should we go?"

"How about Brody's Grill for an after-school snack?" I asked.

"And then we can go to the store," Penny said. "Because I have an idea for Marco's candy. You know those little treats Dad brought home? The mini brownies and cupcakes? We could call them Marco's Minis!"

"That's a GREAT idea," Mom said.

"Yeah, Penny," I said. "You saved the day two times. Maybe you *should* be in charge."

"Not all the time, though, because I'm the middle sister. Sometimes I'm the little one, and sometimes I'm big. When I found Bella, that was a big sister thing to do."

"It sure was," Mom told her.

"I didn't even feel like a five-year-old when I did it. I felt six years old."

"You acted like a six-year-old," Mom told her.

"At least a six-year-old," Penny said. "Maybe even seven. Maybe even eight—like Stella!"

"Don't rush it," Mom said.

"Yeah," I said. "You don't want to be in charge of things. Then you could lose them."

"Like Bella?"

"Uh huh," I said. "It's better not to have a dog at all."

"I thought you wanted a dog," Penny said.

I shook my head. "It's too much responsibility. You might mess up."

"Everyone messes up sometimes," Mom said. "Even grown-ups."

"Even parents?" Penny asked.

"Sure, even parents," Mom said. "You're not the first person to lose a dog, Stel. It could've happened to anyone. I make mistakes with you kids sometimes. I may have been a little hard on you, Stella, when it came to Bella staying with us."

"That's okay," I said. "I lost her, so I probably shouldn't get to have a dog."

"Well, that's a good thing, because you're not getting one. But a little bit of responsibility is a good thing."

"Like a fish?" Penny asked.

"A fish would be fine," Mom said. "What

if we go to Man's Best Friend after all our other errands and get you each one?"

That's just what we did.

Sneak preview of

Stella Batts

Something Blue

Book

Off We Go

Hey readers, remember me? I'm Stella Batts, and this is my SIXTH book.

I'm going to start this story on a Friday, the last day of school for the week. It was a half day, because the teachers had some conferences to go to. It was also the day I was leaving for Los Angeles.

In case you don't know it, Los Angeles is a city in California. Just like the city I live in, Somers, is a city in California. But California is a looooooong state, and Los Angeles and Somers are at different ends of it, so even though they're in the same state, they're actually far apart.

It was going to take four HOURS to drive to Los Angeles, so it was a good thing I got out of school early. Of course, I'm only eight, so I wasn't going to be the one doing the driving. My dad was. Here's a list of everyone going in our car:

1. Me
2. My younger sister Penny
3. My mom
4. My dad

It was almost my whole entire family, except for my baby brother Marco. He was staying home with Stuart, who babysits sometimes. Also my pet fish, Fudge, had to stay home, and so did Penny's pet fish, Penny Jr.

But the rest of us were going, because my Aunt Laura—that's Mom's younger sister—was having her wedding. All my friends knew about our trip. After school that day, when we're saying good-bye, my friend Lucy called out, "Bye, Stella! I hope you have fun with your first first cousin!"

I've never had a cousin before—at least not a first one. That's because Dad's an only child, so I don't have any uncles or aunts on his side of the family. Mom has Aunt Laura, but so far she hasn't had any kids.

Except now she's getting married to a man named Mitch Perlman. He was married before and he has a kid! Her name is Lia. She's nine years old—one year older than I am—

and as soon as her dad marries my aunt, we'll be cousins.

I'd met Soon-to-be Uncle Mitch before, when he and Aunt Laura came to visit Somers. But I hadn't met my one and only soon-to-be cousin yet!

"Thanks!" I called back to Lucy. "I will!"

"I hope you have fun being a flower girl," Arielle said. She's another one of my friends, and she was talking softly, the way she always does.

"Thank you, Arielle," I said.

"I was supposed to be a flower girl once," she said. "But I changed my mind. I didn't want everyone looking at me, and I was afraid I'd trip on my dress when I walked down the aisle."

Tripping on your dress as you walked down the aisle. I hadn't thought about that.

Luckily my dress was too short to trip on. But I had new shoes. Maybe they'd be too slippery. Or maybe wouldn't fit quite right, and I'd fall and scrape up my knees, like I did the day my friend Evie's dog got away.

"Hey, Stella," Talisa said, interrupting what I was thinking inside my head. "Will you remember me in a second?"

"Yup," I said.

"What about in a minute?"

"I'll remember you in a minute, too," I told her.

"Will you remember me after the weekend when you're back home?" she asked.

"Of course, I will," I said.

"Knock knock," she said.

"Who's there?" I asked.

"Oh no, you forgot me already!"

Talisa is always telling knock-knock

jokes, so I should've known. "That's really funny," I told her. "I think it's my favorite one of all."

"All right, children," Mr. King said. "Off we go."

Courtney Sheinmel

Courtney Sheinmel is the author of several books for middle-grade readers, including *Sincerely* and *All The Things You Are*. Like Stella Batts, she was born in California and has a younger sister. However, her parents never owned a candy store. Now Courtney lives in New York City, where she has tasted all the cupcakes in her neighborhood. She also makes a delicious cookie brownie graham-cracker pie. Visit her at www.courtneysheinmel. com, where you can find the recipe along with information about all the Stella Batts books.

Jennifer A. Bell

Jennifer A. Bell is an illustrator whose work can be found on greeting cards, magazines, and almost a dozen children's books. She lives in Minneapolis, Minnesota, with her husband and son. Visit her online at www. JenniferABell.com.

In this early chapter book series, the ups and downs of Stella's life are charmingly chronicled. She's in third grade, she wants to be a writer, and her parents own a candy shop. Life should be sweet, right?

Praise for Stella Batts:

Other books in this series:

Stella Batts Needs a New Name

Stella Batts: Hair Today, Gone Tomorrow

Stella Batts: Pardon Me

Stella Batts A Case of the Meanies

Meet Stella and friends online at www.stellabatts.com